Also by Maria Leach

RIDDLE ME, RIDDLE ME, REE

HOW THE PEOPLE SANG THE MOUNTAINS UP

WHISTLE IN THE GRAVEYARD

Folktales to Chill Your Bones

MARIA LEACH

Illustrated by Ken Rinciari

The Viking Press New York

ACKNOWLEDGMENT

"'Tain't So" ("The Man Who Wouldn't Believe He was Dead")
reprinted by permission of Russell & Volkening, Inc.,
as agents for the author.
First published in 1974 by The Viking Press, Inc.
625 Madison Avenue, New York, N.Y. 10022
Published simultaneously in Canada by
The Macmillan Company of Canada Limited
Printed in U.S.A.

2 3 4 5 78 77 76 75

LIBRARY OF CONGRESS CATALOGING IN PUBLICATION DATA
Leach, Maria. Whistle in the graveyard.
SUMMARY: A collection of folktales from around the world
about ghosts, bogeys, witches, and other haunts. Bibliography: p.
1. Tales. 2. Ghost stories. [1. Folklore. 2. Ghost stories]
I. Rinciari, Ken, illus. II. Title. PZ8.1.L36Wh 398.2'5 73-22255

ISBN 0-670-76245-8

For MARION and DONALD ROBERTSON
M.L.

To my daughter ADRIA
—be kind to the ghosts in your life
K.R.

Contents

WHISTLE IN THE GRAVEYARD

DON'T WORRY

Some people say that ghosts don't seem to hang around nowadays as much as they used to. They say this is because so many wonderful, old, gloomy, empty houses, which ghosts used to haunt, are being torn down, and big shiny high-risers are going up in their places. There are not very many lonely country roads left either for ghosts to wander and wait in; they are all being paved, and traffic goes roaring through. Some people even say that ghosts are afraid of automobiles!

But—DON'T WORRY.

Our ghosts are still there.

All this change does not seem to bother them very much. There are stories of haunted apartments and haunted hotel rooms, where murders have taken place. There are even stories of haunted automobiles; ghostly old Fords and jalopies and hot rods have been reported dashing about all across the continent.

In fact, there are more ghostly hitchhikers than ever in the United States and Canada. Some ghostly hitchhiker haunts some turnpike crossroad in every state in the Union; and no matter how many ghostly hitchhiker stories are known, there is always a new one that has just cropped up somewhere. The story of the ghostly hitchhiker is usually about the pretty girl in the road late at night in her party dress, who hitches a ride with a stranger and asks to be taken home. The stranger drives to the given address; the girl disappears just as they stop before the house. The father (or mother) who comes to the door tells the stranger about the daughter who was killed in an accident on that crossroad on that highway and who keeps trying to come home.

There are stories, too, of a solitary man or woman who boards a bus late at night, only to vanish just before it crosses a bridge. It is well known, of course, that ghosts cannot cross running water; but this poor ghost gets on the same bus time and time again, perhaps always hoping to get across the bridge.

Another ghostly hitchhiker, usually a man, stands at the entrance to a bridge near Goldsboro, North Carolina, and never accepts a lift. He tries to hitch a ride with cars that come along; but if someone stops to pick him up, he disappears.

All the famous ghost ships are still seen at their appointed times: for instance, the *Palatine,* off Block Island, and the *Teazer* in Mahone Bay, off the south shore of Nova Scotia, return to enact their destruction year after year. People also still search for buried treasure, more often than you think; and terrifying things continue to happen to prevent their getting it. Very few people ever see the traditional treasure-guarding ghost; but everyone says he is there.

Mr. Thomas Surette of Yarmouth, Nova Scotia, was approached by a well-dressed gentleman ghost one day and told to dig for treasure on one of the Tusket Islands off the south shore. He knew the gentleman was a ghost because he disappeared when he finished speaking.

Mr. Surette made two attempts to find this treasure, accompanied by his sons; but they were thwarted both times. As they walked through the thick woodsy approach to the spot they were seeking, trees fell across their path, just missing first one, then another of the party; one man fell into a deep pit that suddenly opened before them. The last time they went to the little island seeking the treasure, in 1971, three or four hundred crows kept flying round their heads; and when they thrust their shovels into the earth, there was no bottom to the holes. So they gave up.

That well-dressed ghost certainly wanted Tom Surette to have the treasure, but perhaps Mr. Surette does not know the age-old formula for success in digging treasure. Every treasure hunter must remember that the digger must not speak while digging; he must not laugh; and he must not sweat. Good luck to Tom Surette when he tries again!

Most of the ghosts in this book are still seen from time to time: Anne Boleyn still walks the Tower of London with her head tucked under her arm. The ghosts in the White House in Washington, D.C., still appear to those who are able to see or hear them. The headless man still stands at the end of some big or little bridge, *just staring at you,* at many and many a river or little creek all over the South. The man on Morvan's Road was seen again last week in Shelburne, Nova Scotia. Tony still comes to play his harp in the old house in Southport, North Carolina. People say the drowned still keep trying to come home, leaving bits of seaweed where they stood or a little puddle, like old Captain Boyd in Shelburne, Nova Scotia. And we often still hear that a dead friend or lover or relative has appeared to someone he loves in order to announce his own death, like Grandpa Joe's brother.

This kind of ghost—the apparition of a living person in his exact image, usually seen just before or at the moment of death—is called a *wraith* in England, the United States, and parts of Canada. It is called a *forerunner* in Nova Scotia and Newfoundland, because it predicts or announces the death of its own living double. It is a *fetch* or a *taise* in Ireland, a *Doppelgänger* (double-goer) in Germany. To see one's own wraith is usually taken as an omen of death.

If you want to *prove* that our ghosts are still here, they say you can summon them by calling them by name or just by whistling in a graveyard—*I dare you!* If one comes and you want to get rid of it, just hold up a mirror, and it will run away. Ghosts are afraid of ghosts, they say, and will run from their own reflections!

Famous Ghosts

WHITE HOUSE GHOSTS

The White House must be the most thoroughly haunted house in the United States. Eight ghosts are well known; and many very strange things have been seen or heard. President Truman, for instance, opened his bedroom door two or three times to insistent rappings, and there was nobody there.

Probably the oldest ghost in the White House is Abigail Adams, wife of John Adams, second president of the United States. Although the cornerstone of the White House was laid in 1792, the first tenants, John and Abigail Adams, did not move in until 1800.

The famous East Room was not finished even then. So Abigail used to hang her wash up to dry in there. Several people have seen her going in or coming out of the East Room in her quaint colonial dress; but no one evidently has ever looked to see if the ghost of a clothes-line were there or if any of John Adams' shirts were hanging on it.

The most famous of the White House ghosts is Abraham Lincoln. Lincoln paces the floor of his bedroom on the second floor, they say, on the *night before* any threatened great calamity to the United States actually happens. This worried tread was heard on the night before the United States entered World War I and again on the eve of World War II.

Several people have seen Lincoln back to, standing

in the window of his bedroom, looking out over the Potomac River toward Virginia, just as he used to when some battle was at stake over there between the Union and Confederate armies. Eleanor Roosevelt saw Lincoln sitting on the edge of his bed pulling on his boots one day as she passed his bedroom door. Queen Wilhelmina of the Netherlands said she met Lincoln one evening in the hall while she was visiting in the White House.

One afternoon the whole household was in a flurry because Dolly Madison had been seen in the garden. She was walking distractedly from flower bed to flower bed, looking for something. Then someone remembered that Dolly Madison had planted the first rose beds at the White House. "She is looking for her own roses," someone said—and true enough! That very morning the rose beds had been dug up and transplanted. Once Dolly found them, safe and growing in another spot, she went away and has not been seen since.

Dolly Madison's little cat is a famous ghost, too. It has often been seen curled up in the sun on a window seat or just running around somewhere.

Other famous and recorded stories are that Andrew Jackson has been heard laughing in bed! Abe Lincoln's wife, Mary Todd Lincoln, said she heard Andrew Jackson swearing. Thomas Jefferson has been heard playing the violin. Even an old janitor named Jerry Smith has been seen wandering through the White House with his feather duster.

Occasionally a Mr. Burns (who donated the eighteen acres of land for the White House in 1790) announces himself, unseen, out of the air. "I'm Mister Burns!" he says. "I'm Mister Burns!"

Somebody should do something for Mr. Burns to put his soul at rest. They should put up a plaque for him, or hold a memorial service, or something. He deserves it.

EARL GERALD

Gerald, Fourth Earl of Desmond, who lived in County Limerick in Munster, Ireland, in the late fourteenth century, still lives today, people say, under the deep waters of Lake Gur. He owned the great castle of Mullaghmast nearby in the fierce times when the English were in the midst of trying to rule Ireland. Earl Gerald and his fighting men were strong against them.

Some people say that Earl Gerald sleeps in a cave with his warriors under Castle Mullaghmast and will rise again to drive the English out of Munster. But most people believe that he lives under Lake Gur, for he is seen, every seven years, to rise out of it.

Every seven years Earl Gerald rises from the lake on a shining white horse and rides around the edge of it in the moonlight. Then he rides all over his wide lands to see if all is well in Munster.

The horse wore silver shoes an inch thick when Earl Gerald first disappeared into the lake. When they are worn as thin as a cat's ear, he will come forth to rout the English out of all Ireland forever.

ANNE BOLEYN

Anne Boleyn was the young wife of Henry VIII of England and mother of Queen Elizabeth I. Anne was a beautiful girl, witty and learned and full of fun, a fearless horsewoman, a writer and singer of songs, and the life and delight of every group she was in.

King Henry fell in love with Anne when she was fourteen years old. He had her brought to court as a lady-in-waiting for his wife, Catherine of Aragon; but Henry's mind and heart became more and more enthralled day by day with the brilliant, vivacious girl, until he finally divorced Catherine and married Anne.

His love did not survive the birth of a girl child, however. Henry wanted a son to be king of England after him. So he arranged to get rid of Anne.

She was arrested and charged with treason and imprisoned in the Tower of London—in the section called the Bloody Tower. She declared herself innocent, and many believed in her but dared not oppose the inevitable condemnation. Less than three weeks after her arrest, there in the courtyard of the Tower, Anne was beheaded, with a shining ax, on May 19, 1536.

Ever since that day, it is said, the ghost of Anne returns to protest her innocence, carrying her head in the crook of her arm. She has been seen in the chapel of Saint Peter de Vincula in the Tower (where she is buried), walking in a procession of the dead. Every year on May 19, she appears by herself, lonely and unhappy, at midnight in the Bloody Tower with her head tucked under her arm.

Anne also returns every year on her execution day to Blickling Hall in Norfolk, her childhood home. She comes at night in a coach drawn by four headless horses, driven by a headless coachman. She herself sits inside the coach holding her head in her lap. The coach comes up to the very door and stops—and vanishes.

Out of this sad story came a comic English music-hall song, which was featured by both Gracie Fields and Noel Coward.

Now in the Tower of London, large as life,
The ghost of Anne Boleyn walks, I declare,
Young Anne Boleyn was once King Henry's wife
Until he had the axman bob her hair.
Oh, yes, he done her wrong long years ago,
And back she comes each year to tell him so.

With her head tucked under her arm,
She walks the Bloody Tower
With her head tucked under her arm,
She walks the midnight hour.

Don't Run

WHITE GHOSTS

White Ghosts can run faster than anybody. You can't see their feet when they run. . . . If you see a white ghost, don't run. Just hide. If you run, it will chase you, and if it spits on you, nothing will be left of you but bones.

SKULL RACE

One night a man was sitting all alone in his little house, resting after a hard day's work. Suddenly a human skull rolled across the floor and jumped up on his knee. It stared and grinned at him.

The man was so scared he jumped out of his chair and ran. The skull followed, bouncing along behind him and making a sort of hollow sound. When the man ran, the skull bounced along faster and faster after him; when he stopped, it stopped and waited. When he ran, there it was bouncing, bouncing right at his heels.

The man turned and tried to grab it, but it bounced to the right. He tried again and it bounced to the left.

No use. The man finally gave up and lit out for home. He leaped in and slammed the door. In a minute he looked out the window. The skull was gone.

NOBODY HERE BUT YOU AND ME

One night a man was sitting by his fireplace. He was getting sleepy from the warmth and from watching the fire.

Suddenly a Thing got up out of the fireplace and sat down in a chair beside him. Man didn't say anything. Thing didn't say anything. Nothing happened. They just sat.

Then the Thing said, "Ain't nobody here but you and me."

The man jumped out of his chair, leaped out the door, and RAN. The Thing ran after him.

"Ain't nobody round here running like this but you and me," it hollered after him.

The man ran faster. Got way ahead. He came to a high wall fence and leaned against it to get his breath.

"Ain't nobody leaning on this wall here tonight but you and me," said the Thing.

The man quick clambered up the wall and sat on top of it.

"Ain't nobody sitting on top of this wall but you and me," said the Thing.

The man was so scared he fell off the wall; and the Thing fell off right on top of him.

"Ain't nobody falling down like this but you and me," was the last thing he heard.

Somebody came along the next morning, found the man lying there, and helped him get up and go home.

WHAT'S THE MATTER?

Once there was a brave young fellow who was not afraid of ghosts. He didn't believe in ghosts, he said, "It's all storybook stuff."

So the bunch of boys he was with dared him to go spend the night—*all night*—in a certain haunted house down the road.

He said, "Sure, I'll go stay all night in that old empty house." The boys walked down the road with him to the place. He went in and they went on.

While he was sitting there, in a nice room, waiting for nothing to happen, a pair of legs suddenly came running downstairs. Then a body came bumping down and lay there on the floor. Then a big, smiling head bounced down the stairs, step by step—bounce by bounce!

The young fellow sat there and watched. He was scared all right.

When the body began to put itself together, he just jumped up and ran. He ran out the door and headed for home—fast!—and—of course, the ghostly thing ran after him.

The boy had a good start, so he looked back. The ghost was coming. He ran faster. He looked back again. The ghost was catching up.

Just as he turned into his own yard, it was upon him! It said, "What's the matter? Don't you *like* me?"

The Kind That Won't Stay Dead

OLD TOM COMES HOME

I know when I was a kid we had an old cat and wanted to get rid of 'im. My daddy he hauled him off to town. It was ten miles to town. We was ridin' in a wagon. We took 'im down to town and turned him loose. We carried him across the Yadkin River and over to the North Wilkesboro side and turned him loose.

Well, when we got back home, the blame cat was settin' at home on the porch. And Dad said, "I will fix him," so he got him a sack and put him in it the next time he went to town, and he got him some big rocks, and he put the rocks in the sack and tied the old cat up in the sack and throwed him in the river.

And when we got home, he's a-settin' on the porch, as wet as he could be, and I don't know how he got out of that sack.

Dad told me, he said, "Well, you've got to see if you can't get rid of that cat."

And I said, "Why, I can get rid of him easy."

So I took the old cat way down in the woods. There's a big stump down there, and I took my ax with me. I just laid him down on that stump and chopped his head off. Went on back to the house, we's settin' there on the porch talkin', and in about an hour I looked out the road and there come that cat!

He come out of the woods and was trottin' out the road with his head in his mouth.

'TAIN'T SO

Old Mr. Dinkins was very ill, so they sent for the doctor. When the doctor came, old man Dinkins said, "There's nothing the matter with me!"

"You are dying," said the doctor.

"'Tain't so!" said old man Dinkins. But the next day he was dead.

So they put the old man in his coffin; they carried him to church and had his funeral; then they carried him to the graveyard and buried him.

The next morning a neighbor passing the graveyard on his way to work saw old man Dinkins sitting on the graveyard fence.

"Hello there! I thought you were dead," said the neighbor.

"'Tain't so!" said old man Dinkins.

The neighbor went and told old Mrs. Dinkins that her husband was sitting on the graveyard fence and said he was *not* dead.

"Pay no attention," said the widow. "He's foolish."

Later on another neighbor passing by the graveyard heard someone say, "Hello, Tom!"

"Hello," said Tom and stopped for a chat. "It's you, is it?"

"Sure," said old man Dinkins.

"I heard you were dead."

"'Tain't so!"

"I heard about the burial."

"Well, you can see I'm not buried."

"That's so," said the neighbor and went on his way, somewhat puzzled.

The next day one of the townsmen was passing by the graveyard on horseback. He heard someone say, "Hello," and stopped to see who it was. He saw a very old gentleman sitting on the fence, who said, "What's the news from town?"

"Not much news, except old man Dinkins is dead."

"'Tain't so!"

"That's what they said."

"Well, 'tain't so."

"How do you know?" said the man.

"I'm Dinkins."

"Oh!" said the man and rode away from the place pretty fast.

He stopped at the next store and said, "There's a funny old fellow sitting on the graveyard fence who says he is old man Dinkins."

"Can't possibly be," said the storekeeper.

"Why not?"

"Because old man Dinkins is dead."

This kept going on week after week, month after month. The whole town knew that old man Dinkins was dead; but old man Dinkins sat on the graveyard fence saying, "'Tain't so."

After much talk and consultation the townspeople decided to hold *another* burial service.

So they said the burial service over the old man's grave for a second time and set up his gravestone.

The words on the gravestone said:

Here Lies the Body of
Theodore Dinkins
aged 91
Respected citizen of
Wadmalaw Island
who died
January 17, 1853

The next day when old man Dinkins crawled out of his grave, he read what the stone said. He read it over two or three times.

"Well—maybe so," he said. He hasn't yelled at anybody from the graveyard fence since then.

Treasure Ghosts

ONE HANDFUL

"My grandfather told the story," said Mr. Wilkins, "about a man who came to him in a dream and told about a big iron box under a silk-cotton tree way up the Supanaan River. The iron box was full of gold, the dream ghost told him.

"'But take only one handful!' the ghost said, 'or something horrible will happen to you.'

"My grandfather did not go looking for the gold. He would go some day, he thought; but it was a long, perilous trip up the river in that wild country, and why bother, for only one handful of gold? He told the story to his son, however, just before he died.

"The son, too, did not seek the treasure. He also thought the journey was too long and too difficult for only one handful of gold. This man, too, before he died, told *his* son about the grandfather's dream.

"This grandson had grown up to be a more worldly and ambitious man than either his father or grandfather. He thought about the gold a lot—all that gold, hidden in a box under a tree.

"He wanted it—so he decided to go and get it—and no silly, old, long-forgotten, superstitious warning was going to limit him to one handful, either. He wanted it all.

"He made the trip alone up the river in safety. He found the wonderful, lucky silk-cotton tree. He dug into the roots and soon found the iron box. It was rusty, but he got it open. It was filled with gold, filled to the brim.

"He plunged both hands in—to take double. The lid of the box slammed down!"

Mr. Wilkins paused. Some minutes went by. "What happened?" said the listener.

In answer Mr. Wilkins suddenly thrust out his two arms. *Both hands were gone.*

CAN'T REST

Once there was an old man in Wayne County, Missouri, who had a rich farm, and everybody said he had hidden away a great fortune. He was murdered one night as he sat by the fire in his house by somebody who wanted his money. After that people used to see his ghost wandering over the fields or going in and out the door of the house. Nobody would live in the house. Nobody would go near the place.

One evening an old tired traveler came through the village, saw the empty house, and decided to stop for the night. He went in and built a big fire and fell asleep in the chair by the fireplace in the nice warmth.

In the middle of the night he suddenly woke up and saw another old man sitting facing him in another chair in front of the fire.

"I can't rest," said the old fellow. "I can't rest! You follow me and I'll show you where the money is." So the old traveler got up and followed the ghost out into the yard.

"Can't rest till somebody finds the money," the ghost said again.

They walked around the house to where the old stone chimney rose up alongside the house. The old ghost pulled out some little stones and then one big stone at the base of the chimney.

"It's in there," he said.

So the traveler reached his arm in and pulled out a bundle wrapped in dirty old newspapers. It was full of money.

After that nobody ever saw the ghost again.

BLACKBEARD'S TREASURE

Old Edward Teach, the famous pirate, was usually called Blackbeard. He buried his fabulous treasure in the marshlands along Pamlico River in North Carolina, somewhere near a little town named Hobucken. The treasure is in a chest, the local people say, and alongside the chest old Blackbeard buried a man to take care of it.

Many people have found the place: a deep pit in the marsh, lined with bricks; but nobody has ever been able to get the treasure—yet. Something always happens to terrify the seeker; and of course, once he gives up or runs away, he can never find the place again.

One man who found the place cleared the marsh grass away and got his hand down far enough to feel the bricks. Then something blew ice-cold down the back of his neck. He began to shake. So he thought he would clear a good path from there to the road. And then he went home to get a wheelbarrow. When he got back with the wheelbarrow, the marsh grass had already grown waist high again. He searched and searched, but he never could find the right spot again.

Another man later also found the place and thought he would mark the spot for sure. He ran a stake into the mud and hung his shirt on it. A strong icy wind began to blow—on a hot night. At every move he made the grass grabbed his feet. He decided to go home and get a shovel, and the grass let him go. When he got back with the shovel, the stake and the shirt were gone. This man too searched and searched but could not find them. The tall grasses rippled in the wind, and he shook with a fatal, icy chill. The marsh was as lonely as ever. That night the man died.

There have been many seekers, even many finders, but no one has lifted up the treasure yet. Those who live nearby often hear the poor old ghost who guards the treasure singing sea songs in the night in the wind.

THE TIRED GHOST

Long ago a shipload of pirates landed at Bonavista, Newfoundland, and buried "immense treasure," legend says, somewhere on the great eastern beach of Bonavista Bay. Then they went off to get more.

They left one man on grim and solemn oath never to leave it unguarded until they returned.

Years went by. The pirates never came back. The poor fellow left behind grew old—grew old and died, but his ghost is there.

The ghost still guards the treasure. Nobody has dared to dig it up. One or two men tried, years ago, but were terrified and went mad or were killed in the attempt. After that no one has dared to risk it.

Now the poor old ghost is tired of his vigil. He wishes someone *would* dig up the treasure so he can rest.

One night he stopped a fisherman who was walking along the beach on his way home. Casually, as if he were discussing fishing weather, he said, "Come here alone at midnight, shed blood on this spot, and you can have the treasure. The blood," he explained, can be chicken blood or a few drops out of your own wrist."

The fisherman was scared to death and hurried home without answering. The old ghost has stopped and said the same thing to many, many people, but everyone is too scared to try it.

Everybody knows, of course, that the ghost is honor bound to scare people off, even though he really wants somebody brave enough to come along and dig up the treasure.

Why don't you try it?

Cauld, Cauld

CAULD, CAULD, FOREVER CAULD

The Cauld (cold) Lad at Gilsland in Cumberland, England, is the ghost of a little boy who died of cold. He was shut up in a closet upstairs for some childish misbehavior. It was winter and there was no heat in the bare upstairs rooms of the great house. The little boy froze to death.

His ghost wanders from room to room, shivering, teeth chattering, looking for a warm place.

Everybody tries to keep him out of the bedrooms, because he comes to the side of the bed and lays his cold hand on you. The hand is so cold that you never feel warm again.

If he comes to the bedside of someone very ill and touches the hot face, he says:

Cauld, cauld, forever cauld,
You shall be cauld forever more.

The person dies soon after that.

THE OUTSIDE MAN

These two stories about the Outside Man were written by two school children on Umnak Island (in the Aleutian Islands) many years ago. The teacher had said, "Tomorrow you must hand in a story written in your own words." This meant a story *written in English,* of course, for this was a small school for Aleutian Eskimo children learning English.

Martin, who was eleven, handed in a ghost story about the *asx̣athax̣.* The *asx̣athax̣* is the ghost of a dead relative or village neighbor. The word means "Outside Man." The people call him that because he is always trying to come in out of the cold. He is jealous of their warmth and tries to do harm, especially to children.

Sometimes the Outside Man throws rocks or ice-balls at people or trips them in the snow with thongs of strong dry grass. His pockets are full of sleet. He throws handfuls of sleet in people's faces, biting, stinging sleet, to blind them so he can take hold of them. He even climbs on the roofs of houses during windstorms and snaps the roofing off, hoping the children will run out to see what is the matter so he can catch them.

Here is Martin's story.

One time I saw an *asx̣athax̣* on the beach. Robert was with me. There were two of them walking along the beach. They waved their caps at us. We waved back, but I was afraid and ran home fast.

Here is Christina's story. She was fourteen years old.

One day a man went out to set traps and took his two little boys with him. They came to the camping place. They put up their tent and built a fire.

The father was chopping wood for the fire. Something began to throw snow rocks at him. He looked around, but no one was there.

Suddenly he was afraid that the Outside Man was nearby and would get into the tent and carry off the two little boys. So he ran to the tent.

The Outside Man was in there. He was walking around the tent and staring at the two little boys.

The man went into the tent and lay down and pretended to be dead asleep. The Outside Man paid no attention to him. It was the two little boys he was after.

Suddenly the father jumped up and ran at the Outside Man. "I'll GET you!" he roared.

The Outside Man was so surprised he just ran off!

So the father and the two little boys packed up their things and went home. The two little boys tried not to cry.

"He was bad! He was awful!" said one.

"I was scared," said the other.

I'M COMING UP THE STAIRS

Once there was a little girl named Tilly who was afraid to go to bed. Nothing bad had ever happened to her, but somebody had told her some scary stories, and after that she was afraid.

One night she really did hear something. She lay in bed—listening—and she heard a very quiet voice say, "Tilly, I'm coming up the stairs."

The next night Tilly asked her mother if she could keep the light on for a while, but her mother said, "Nonsense, darling." Nothing happened that night, so Tilly did not ask again. But the next night while Tilly was lying in bed, afraid to go to sleep, she heard a little voice say, slowly, "Tilly, I'm on the first step."

Tilly was too scared to get up and look.

The next night she heard the little whispering voice say, "Tilly, I'm on the second step."

Tilly got more and more scared each night, but everybody told her, "Oh, that's nothing."

There were eight steps in the staircase; and every night Tilly heard the voice.

"Tilly, I'm on the third step"—

"Tilly, I'm on the fourth step"—

"Tilly, I'm on the fifth step"—until one night she heard the voice say, "Tilly, I'm in the hall."

Tilly was so frightened she couldn't eat her breakfast the next morning, and she couldn't eat her supper that night.

The next night Tilly was lying awake in bed, and it was not very long before she heard that horrid little whispering voice say, "Tilly, I'm at the door."

The next night it said, "Tilly, I'm *in the room!*"

Tilly was too scared even to scream for her mother.

The next night the voice said, "Tilly, I'm standing by the bed!" And the next night

I'VE GOT YOU!

THE MAN ON MORVAN'S ROAD

Morvan's Road runs through thick woods from Shelburne south to Jordan Bay on the South Shore of Nova Scotia. Nobody uses it much any more. The alders are closing in. It is hard for cars to pass through.

The Allen sisters, two elderly ladies of Shelburne town, tell of driving a few years ago with a group of people in two cheerful wagonloads to a Sunday School convention in Jordan Ferry.

That evening at dusk they were driving back through Morvan's Road, when suddenly the horses stopped and refused to move on. The driver looked ahead and saw a man in the road walking toward them.

The driver stopped as the man came alongside the wagon.

"Can we give you a lift?" said the driver.

The man did not answer. He leaned his arms on the side of the wagon, then leaned his head in toward the people and gazed earnestly into each face. He did not speak.

The chill and silence of the night woods seemed to close in around them.

The man walked then to the second wagon and did the same thing. Without speaking he leaned in and looked searchingly into each face, as if seeking someone lost. In a moment he vanished.

The people were stunned and frightened, but the horses were eager to go on, and the party drove toward home.

"I've heard of the man on Morvan's Road," said one man, "but I never saw him before."

When the two sisters were going to bed that night, one said, "Well, we've seen old man Morvan."

"Poor fellow," said the other.

A lot of people have had such experiences. Anyone walking through Morvan's Road at night or at early dusk is likely to meet up with old man Morvan. He steps out of the bushes at the side of the road and walks alongside a lone traveler. He never speaks; he just walks along, looks into the face of the person, and then suddenly is not there.

Some people do not mind and just go along with the poor lonely ghost. Some are scared to death and never walk that road again. Today a young man from Shelburne came to my house, and I asked him how many miles long Morvan's Road was. "I don't know," he said. "I've only been in there once, and I'm afraid to go again."

STARING AT YOU!

Willeena was fifteen years old, pretty and smart. She was devoted to the two little boys she took care of. Their mother taught school, and Willeena came every morning to play with the two boys and give them their lunch.

Every morning she walked about a mile from her house to the Yarbrough house, and in the evening she walked back home again. The path ran through backyard gardens, through a stretch of dark woods, and over a big plank that crossed a little creek.

One day when Willeena came, she looked kind of big-eyed and scared. She didn't sing that day. She didn't laugh or jump around or play games as she usually did.

Willeena was like that for two or three days: scared and silent and sort of shaky.

The next day she asked Mrs. Yarbrough if she could go home early. "Before dark," she said.

Mrs. Yarbrough thought Willeena must surely be sick and said, "Yes, of course."

It was fall and the late afternoons were getting dark earlier and earlier. Each day Willeena kept begging to go home earlier and earlier. "Before dark," she said.

"What's the matter, Willeena?" asked Mrs. Yarbrough finally. "Why do you want to go so early?"

"Oh, ma'am, there's a man," she said. "There's a man stands by the creek. He got no head!"

"Well, what does he do?"

"He don't do nothing. He just stands there staring at you."

"But how can a man stare at you if he doesn't have any head?"

"I don't know, ma'am, but he does it!" cried Willeena. "He just stands there in the dark staring at you!"

THE SEA CAPTAIN AT THE DOOR

It was a foggy spring night in Shelburne, Nova Scotia. The fog moved up the long harbor from the sea and shrouded the little town in mystery, as vast sea fogs always do. Each house was folded into its own secrets.

About ten o'clock, when Marion Robertson went to the front door to put out the milk bottle, the fog had closed in. As she opened the door she was aware of a man standing in the entry. He was wearing a sea-captain's uniform of years ago, and he was soaking wet.

The man did not say a word. He just stood there a minute, gazing into the cozy hall, and vanished.

"It must be old Captain Boyd," Marion thought.

She walked back to the warm kitchen. She had no fear, but she began to remember the story.

Old John Boyd had owned the house about a hundred years ago, and his son, Captain Michael Boyd, was lost at sea. His ship had burned to the water in a heavy gale. Other ships had stood by, hoping to rescue the crew as they jumped into the sea to escape the flames. As the onlookers watched the burning ship, they saw a woman (it was Mrs. Boyd) and the Captain struggle out onto the tip of the bowsprit; they saw the flames take the bowsprit, and it fell into the sea.

"Yes. He just wanted to come home," Marion said to herself. "The drowned always want to come home."

The next morning as she left the house to do her errands, she noticed a little pool of water in the entry way where the man had stood.

GRANDPA JOE'S BROTHER

Grandpa Joe's brother's name was Wilfred. Grandpa Joe himself was Captain Joseph Wickens, an old-time fisherman of Bear Point, Nova Scotia, skilled in the ways of sail, hauling nets, and dory hand-trawling.

Young Wilfred, too, was a fisherman, sailing on a schooner out of Gloucester, Massachusetts. In those days there were few radios or telephones, and once Wilfred was at sea, there was no chance to send a message. His family seldom knew where Wilfred was.

One clear evening young Joe left his house, on the west side of Bear Point, to walk up to Stoddart's store on some errand for his young wife. As he walked along, he saw a fisherman in the road ahead of him in high rubber boots and billed cap. The figure stopped a moment in the faint light of a neighbor's window, and Joe recognized his brother.

"Wilfred," he called. "Wilfred."

Wilfred's vessel must have come in, Joe thought, for supplies, or repairs, or shelter; and Wilfred would be home for the night!

"Wilfred," he called again. "Wilfred!"

The figure ahead turned and looked at him but made no answer. Joe saw his brother's face and called his name once more—and the figure vanished.

Joe turned and went back home. At the sight of him when he entered the house, his young wife, Luella, cried, "Joe! What's wrong?"

"Something is going to happen to Wilfred," he said. "I have just seen his forerunner." And he wept.

The next morning Joe did not leave the house. He sat in a chair by the window and waited for the news he knew must come. About noon his youngest brother came across Bear Point (from the old home on the east side) by a path through the woods. Luella ran out of the house to meet him.

"Have you come about Wilfred?" she asked.

"Yes," the boy answered. "How did you know?"

"Joe saw his forerunner last night. He's waiting for word to come."

That night there had been a terrific gale off shore with rising seas. The Gloucester schooner had tried to make Shelburne Harbor for shelter; and the Gloucester captain had mistaken Sandy Point light for Shelburne light. Wilfred was the only Nova Scotia seaman on board who had ever taken a vessel into Shelburne Harbor. He tried to warn the captain that he was not where he thought he was!

The warning went unheeded. The schooner struck a ledge and was held on the rocks by the force of the wind. The crew were able to launch one dory, and three men got safe ashore. Other dories could have been launched, but one man, in a panic, seized an ax and cut the stays holding the foresail, thinking this might save the vessel. Instead she heeled over and broke up, drowning twenty-four men.

BILL IS WITH ME NOW

Many years ago in the slave-trade era, there was an old sailor named Bill Jones on board a slave vessel from Liverpool, England. The captain of the vessel was a man of violent temper, violent dislikes, and fits of cruelty. He took a great dislike to Bill Jones, who was growing old and slowing up.

One day because the old fellow seemed slower than usual getting out on a yardarm to handle sail, the captain cursed and abused him; then, in a final spurt of rage, he shot him.

The sailors carried old Bill down from the yard. As he lay dying on the deck, he looked into the captain's face and said, "Yes, you have done me in, but *I will never leave you."*

The captain went right on cursing the old man until he drew his last breath. Then the captain ordered the body thrown into the slave-kettle to be served to the slave cargo as stew.

As time went on, members of the crew began to say that the ghost of old Bill was on board. Several men had seen him. He often performed his own share of a turn of duty, especially if the men were handling sail. In fact, old Bill was usually out on a yardarm at these times before anyone else. Everybody saw him.

The captain saw old Bill's ghost out there too, but he pretended not to. The crew knew the captain saw him, however, because of the look of terror on his face.

The crew were not afraid of Bill's ghost for their own sakes; but they were afraid that something terrible was going to happen.

Finally the captain could not stand having old Bill watch him, constantly watch him any longer. One day he called the mate into his cabin and said, "You heard him, Jack; you heard him say he would *never leave me* —and he hasn't. You see him now and then, but I see him every minute. He is here with me now!"

The mate did not know what to say.

"I am going to leave this ship," said the captain. "I cannot bear it."

The mate tried to calm the captain's fears. "You can't leave the ship in mid-ocean," he said.

"Yes, I can," said the captain. "I intend to."

The mate was then called on deck for a few minutes to attend to some matter, and just as he turned back to finish his conversation with the captain, he heard a splash.

He rushed to the rail of the ship and looked over. The captain was sinking into the sea. He rose once and cried out, "Bill is with me now!" He was never seen again.

TONY AND HIS HARP

There is a huge and beautiful haunted house in Southport, North Carolina. Its ghost's name is Tony, and he has been around, they say, for about one hundred years.

Longer ago than that, the big old place used to be a hotel; and three musicians played in the dining room every night. In the daytime sometimes the three young men used to go fishing; but they were on hand every evening to make music for the guests in the dining room.

One day when they went off fishing, all three were drowned. Dinnertime came, but no musicians appeared. It was a silent meal, for the sad news of the drowning had already reached the dining room.

Then suddenly they heard the harp! Everybody looked up, and there was Tony in his accustomed place playing the lovely, familiar melody that was his specialty. People smiled. Everybody was glad that one of the three had survived.

Then, just as suddenly the music faded; Tony and the harp *were not there*—only a small puddle of water on the floor where he had been. The people panicked and ran out of the house.

The next night Tony came again to play as usual, but he had to be forbidden. The people were terrified and would not enter the dining room.

He still comes back, however. People hear him come into the house and slam the door. They hear light running steps up the stairs—and later the soft melody of the harp can be heard in every room.

The house is still a guest house, and Tony still faithfully comes. Modern transient tourists do not see him; but overnight guests have heard the harp. They say it sounds very thin and far away, but it can be heard clearly in the house.

Ghostly Things

CROSSING THE BRIDGE

One very dark night about 150 years ago, a young traveler walked into the inn at Great Barrington, Massachusetts. The inn stood at the end of a bridge over the Housatonic River.

The innkeeper had known the young man for a number of years and greeted him warmly.

"Where did you cross the river?" he asked.

"Right there—by the bridge," said the traveler.

"Impossible!" said the innkeeper. "It isn't there! There is not a plank on it!"

"But I did," said the young man. "The horse came right over—didn't even hesitate."

The traveler admitted that it was too dark to see. He did not *see* the bridge, but the horse knew the way. "The horse must have seen the bridge because he came right along over it," he said.

Both men were puzzled. Neither one believed the other. When bedtime came, however, they said good-night amicably.

In the morning at breakfast, the inkeeper said to the traveler, "Go take a look at your bridge."

So the young man strolled out to the riverbank and looked.

The bridge was a naked frame—not a plank on it.

THE GHOSTLY SPOOLS

Years ago in old French Canada, in the time when people were still spinning yarn to make their homespun garments, an old grandmother of the village used to hire women of the neighborhood to come to her house to spin and wind the yarn on spools.

One day one of the poor old women stole some of the spools, and very shortly after that she sickened and died.

Soon after the funeral, the old grandmother woke up in the night and heard a noise in the attic over her bedroom. It sounded like wooden spools rolling around on the attic floor.

"I'll go look in the morning," she said to herself.

In the morning she went up to the attic to look around, but she could not see or find anything unusual.

She heard the noise again the next night. It sounded exactly like wooden spools rolling and clattering around on the attic floor. She searched the attic again but found nothing. Every night after that the sound of spools rolling around would wake her up and keep her awake.

Then one night, in the middle of the night, when she heard the spools rolling, she suddenly remembered the poor old neighbor who had stolen some of her spools.

"It must be Lucie," she thought. (That was the old neighbor's name.) "She's bringing them back!"

Quickly she got out of bed and went up the attic stairs; softly she opened the attic door at the top of the stairs; softly she called:

"Lucie, Lucie! Is that you? It's all right, Lucie," she said. "You can have the spools."

At once the sound stopped, and the old grandmother never heard it again.

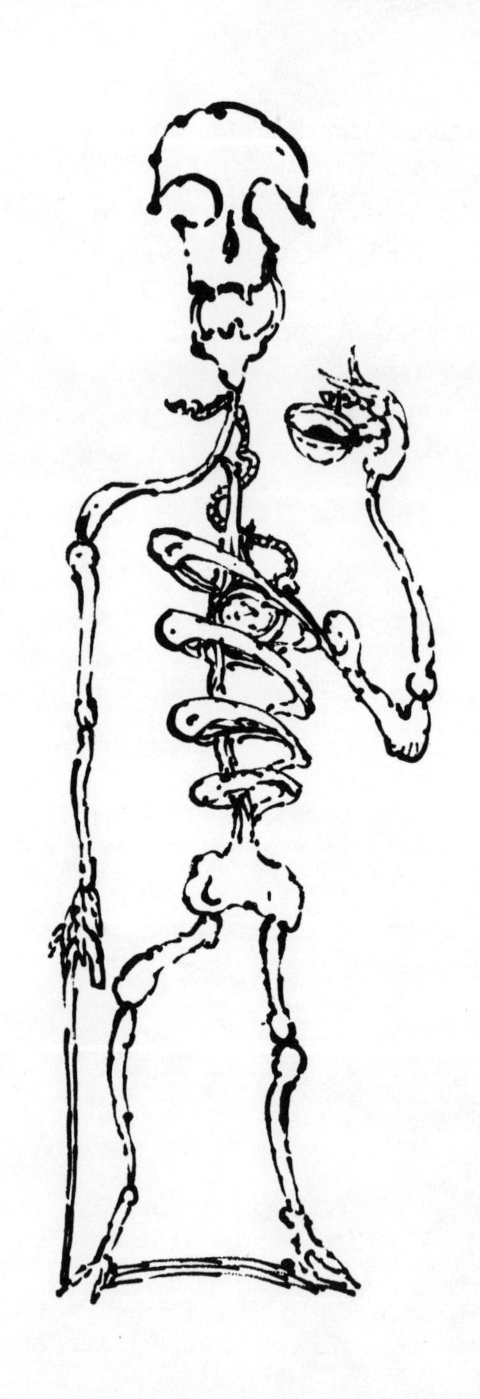

TICK, TICK, TICK

Once there was an old man in New Castle, Delaware, who swallowed a watch. It was a pretty little watch. The old man used to dip it in his sugary tea and lick it or suck on it. It never seemed to hurt the watch. It ticked right along, day in, day out, as a watch should.

One night when the old man was sucking in his sticky, sugary tea in this fashion, all of a sudden, without meaning to, he swallowed the watch!

His old wife put her ear to his gullet and heard it ticking. It was ticking louder than the old man's hiccups. He had the awful hiccups because he could not cough it up and he could not make it slide down.

The old woman sent for the doctor, but the old man died before the doctor got to him. They had the funeral the next day, and the watch ticked louder than the preacher's funeral sermon.

You can go to the old man's grave today, they say, and still hear the watch tick, tick, ticking.

Sometimes children walking by hear it ticking and run away because they think the old man is after them. They think the tick, ticking is the old man's false teeth clicking.

PUMPKIN

Old Grandaddy had a big field of pumpkins down there in Florida. One night somebody came into the field to steal some. Whoever it was took a lot. His name was Joe.

Old Grandaddy heard him and went out the back door and saw him; but he was too old and tired to chase him.

Joe took the pumpkins home and started to cut one up into small slices, the way you cut pumpkins to make a pie. He put the pieces in a pot and put the pot on the stove.

As soon as it was hot, a piece of pumpkin jumped out of the pot onto the floor. Joe picked it up and put it back in the pot. It jumped out again. So he put it back in again. Then the whole pumpkin took to jumping out of the pot, piece by piece, and all the pieces ran around the floor.

Joe picked them all up and put them back in the pot, and they all jumped out again and ran all over the place.

Joe picked them all up *again* and put them back in the pot and put the lid on quick. But they kicked the lid off the pot, and leaped out again, and ran around everywhere.

So Joe picked them all up AGAIN, put them back in the pot, put the lid on quick, then sat on the lid.

He had to sit on the lid about two hours to keep the pumpkin in the pot. The lid got so hot it burned the seat out of his pants.

The next day Joe made a pumpkin pie. He had to stand up to eat it, because he couldn't sit down. He didn't like it much by that time anyway.

Some people say Old Grandaddy was a *conjure man* and had bewitched the pumpkin to punish the thief. And some say you never can tell, around Halloween time, whether a pumpkin is really a pumpkin or just the ghost of some poor old last year's eaten-up pumpkin.

Bogeys and Bugaboos

JENNY GREEN TEETH

Jenny Green Teeth lives in a pond in the bottom of an old gravel pit. Her teeth are scummy and green, and her hair and her long scraggly arms are green too from the thick scum that covers the surface of the pond.

Her arms are long enough to reach out and grab any child that comes too near the edge of the pond, especially if he or she stumbles on a rock and falls down—and ESPECIALLY if children have been told not to go play in the gravel pit, Jenny Green Teeth will grab them and drown them.

Some people say she is the ghost of a little girl who once fell into the pond and was drowned and never got home again. She is lonely, they say, and drags every child she can get hold of into the pond for company.

BABA YAGA

Baba Yaga is a hideous old Russian witch-hag who steals, boils, and eats children. She has one long, long foot on one leg, and the other leg is all bone.

She lives in a little hut that stands on chicken legs. It stands still for a while, then suddenly it turns around, and through the door you can see Baba Yaga.

She lies on her back on the floor with her head at the door, the long, long foot in one corner of the hut and the other foot in the other corner. Sometimes the nose is inside the door, sometimes out—so you can see how long it is.

Baba Yaga is not just a fairy-tale character, however. In old folk belief, it was Baba Yaga who rode through the air in a kettle just ahead of thunderstorms; and the people used to tell their children, "If she comes for you, say nothing. Keep silent." The belief was that if she could make children talk to her, they could not escape her.

NUINUMMA-KWITEN

Nuinumma-Kwiten is the name of a frightening Australian bogey who eats children when they cry. Mothers sing a lullaby that tells how big he is. He swallows ostrich eggs whole; that is how big he is.

The lullaby also says, "I eat crybabies!" He can tell where they are because he can hear them crying.

POT-TILTER

Pot-Tilter is an ugly old hag believed in by the Crow Indians of the North American Great Plains. She carries a boiling pot wherever she goes. When she tilts it toward unwary hunters or children, it sucks them in. Then when they are thoroughly boiled, she eats them for dinner.

Pot-Tilter is not a bedtime bogey called on to hush crying children. She wanders in the woods and bushes near villages, waiting for children who stray too far from home.

Once she tilts the pot toward them, they are pulled into it. No matter how hard they try to run the other way, the pot just draws them to it and sucks them in.

WILLIE WINKIE

Wee Willie Winkie runs through the town
Upstairs, downstairs, in his nightgown,
Rapping at the window, crying through the lock,
"Are the children all in bed?
It's now eight o'clock!"

Willie Winkie is a nursery character, a sort of Sandman who runs through the world at bedtime making children sleepy. He is also a sort of cross between Sandman and bogey, for he too is often called on to frighten children who do not want to go to sleep. There are stories of English nursemaids sticking their heads out of windows and yelling "Hey! Willie Winkie, here's one that's still awake!" The second verse of the famous rhyme reveals this side of his character:

Hey! Willie Winkie: are you coming then?
The cat is singing gray thrums[1] *to the sleepy hen.*
The dog is spread out on the floor and doesn't
give a cheep.
But here's a wakeful laddie who won't go to
sleep!

1. Thrums: humming or purring.

The old Scottish version says:

Hey! Willie Winkie: the wean's[2] *in a creel!*[3]
Wambling[4] *off a body's knee like a very eel!*
Hey! Willie Winkie!—See! Here he comes! . . .

at which point, of course, any small child is supposed to go instantly to sleep!

2. Wean: baby or small child.
3. Creel: spell of fussiness, fidgetiness, or temper.
4. Wambling: squirming around.

RAW HEAD AND BLOODY BONES

Raw Head and Bloody Bones is an ancient bogey who looks exactly like his name. His head is raw bloody flesh, and his hands and arms are nothing but bloody bones. He has been called on to come and frighten crying or disobedient children for over four hundred years. One old book says that English nursemaids used to call his name at bedtime "to terrify crying brats"; but "Raw Head and Bloody Bones will get you!" has been a bedtime word in England, Scotland, the United States, and Canada longer than anyone really knows.

In Kentucky they say he is tall enough to reach his bloody hand-bones into a second-story window and drag out children who won't mind. He is even tall enough to lick salt off the top of a chimney! (He must like salt! Nothing is explained about that.) He lies in wait outdoors, too, for some small child (who would not obey the night before) to come along his path.

In Maine they tell children that one of his hands is withered and tiny like a child's, with blood running out of it, but very strong. The hand can grab a child so he cannot get away; then when he is scared enough to promise to be good forever, old Raw Head and Bloody Bones will let him go.

In Warwickshire, England, if some youngster has been told not to go near the edge of a pool, but *does*—Raw Head and Bloody Bones will drag him in. Then there will be nothing left of that child, either, but raw head and bloody bones.

Witch Lore

THE BLACK CAT'S EYES

Two hunters from the village of Tres Fulgores in New Mexico went hunting one cold winter night up into the hills around Tapia Azul. It snowed all night; the hunters were cold and discouraged and decided to come back home.

It was hard going through the snow, and darkness fell upon them before they could reach their village. So, as they stumbled along, they kept looking for some place to spend the night. After a long time they saw a little light glimmering in the distance, and with stiff weariness they headed for it.

It was late when finally they reached a little house. They knocked on the door, but there was nobody home. They went in anyway, for the door was not locked. They decided to build a good fire in the fireplace. A little black cat was mewing pitifully in the room.

"She's cold, too," said one of the hunters.

"She has no eyes!" said the other. They both stared at the cat and saw that its eye sockets were empty.

The man turned back to building the fire. As he tossed a good stick into the fireplace, his foot touched a little saucer on the hearth. Something in the saucer moved, and he saw two eyes shining up at him. They were *human eyes.*

"Look here!" he cried.

The other man looked.

"They must be witch eyes!" he said and quickly tossed them into the fire.

The two men slept well and warm and got up before daylight. They ate a good breakfast and then waited a little while, hoping to thank the owner of the house for the comfort of the night.

Soon they heard a thump on the roof, then the sound of scrabbling down the chimney.

An old witch landed in the hot coals in the fireplace and screamed! She looked for her eyes in the little saucer, but they were not there. She cursed whoever had taken them, but the two hunters just walked away and never went back there again.

This old witch borrowed her cat's eyes every night so that she could see in the dark, and she always left her own in the little saucer to use the next day.

The little black cat lay crying under the bed, because she knew now that she would never get her own eyes back again.

HOW TO BECOME A WITCH

A man named Nick thought he would like to be a witch. He had heard a lot of stories going around about an old man in the neighborhood called Old Sam who could bewitch people and always got the best of anyone he didn't like.

Nick thought that would be nice, so he went to Old Sam's house and said, "Can you teach me how to be a witch-man like you, so's I can get the best of some awful mean people next door?"

"All right," said Old Sam, "come along outdoors."

The went out in the yard behind the house, and Nick watched Old Sam draw a circle in the dirt with a stick.

"Now you get inside that ring," said Old Sam. "This is a magic ring."

Nick stepped inside the circle.

"Put one hand on top of your head and the other hand under your foot," said Old Sam. So Nick put one hand on top of his head, then stooped down and put the other hand under his foot.

"Now say

Devil take me
Devil take the ring
Devil take me
And everything."

Nick said it.

"Say it again! Sing it!" said Old Sam.

Nick started to, but he was so scared he could hardly get the words out. Just as he got to the part where he said

Devil take me
Devil take the ring

the ground began to sink under his feet. It sank till the edge of the hole was around his knees. He felt himself disappearing right into the earth. When he was down to his hips, he could hear Old Sam laughing his head off. When he was down in to his belt, Nick quick grabbed the edge of the hole and gave himself a great heave back into the world. Then he started to run and never stopped till he got home.

He decided he didn't want to be a witch after all.

Fakes

NEXT TURN TO THE RIGHT

A certain foolish young man, walking through the town streets one evening, stopped and chatted with some passing friends. They told him he looked very ill.

"Oh, no! I'm fine," he said. But as he was walking on alone, he began to think he did feel rather ill.

He began to worry about it, and the more he worried, the worse he felt. He kept feeling worse and worse, and finally he thought he was very near to dying. In a few more minutes he felt so awful he thought he was dead. So he lay down.

Soon a group of passersby came along and saw the young man lying by the side of the walk.

"Is he dead?" said one.

The foolish young man neither moved nor spoke.

"He must be dead," said another. "Go get a bier."

So two of the group went off to get a bier, and two of them waited beside the body.

"I guess it is true," the foolish young man thought to himself. "They think I am dead, too."

Soon the two who had gone off for the bier came back with it. They laid the young man gently upon it and started to carry him to the graveyard. They intended to bury this poor friendless corpse who had died all alone in the street.

When they had gone some distance, they seemed to have lost their way. They stopped to confer but could not agree which way to go.

"Turn right at the next corner," said the foolish young man.

A BREATH OF AIR

One night a man was walking home from visiting a friend and noticed that he was being followed by a small group whom he knew to be robbers. He dodged in and out of alleys, doubled back, turned corners; but he could not shake them off.

Finally he got a little ahead, and as he was passing a graveyard, he noticed a new open grave. So he jumped in! He hid and waited. Nothing happened; he heard no sound. He thought he had escaped them at last and rose up to peek over the edge.

The robbers were coming. They saw his head above the edge of the grave.

"What are you doing in there?" one said.

"This is my grave," said the man. "I just came up for a breath of air."

THE GHOST ON BRASS'S HILL

When Ben Doane was about twelve or thirteen years old, he was living in the small village of fishing boats and sailing ships, in Nova Scotia, called Barrington Passage.

One cold winter evening in 1836, Ben's sister was taken ill, and he was sent off to the doctor—to describe the symptoms and bring back the medicine. It meant a walk of about four and one-half miles to Barrington Head, at the head of Barrington Harbor, where Dr. Geddes lived. The shore road was narrow and banked with snow as high as a man's head.

Young Ben set out undaunted in the cold night, bright enough with snow and stars. About halfway there, he came to Brass's Hill. Old John Brass used to live on Brass's Hill and was buried there somewhere. There were rumors of people seeing and hearing strange things at night.

Ben had been over Brass's Hill time and time again and had never seen or heard anything unusual. He was not worried.

Just as he began the climb up the hill, he saw a man come over the top of it, walking toward him in the narrow path.

He could see the man's shoulders against the white snow—but no head. He could see the legs walking toward him—but no feet. He wanted to run, but there was no escape on either side of the road between the two high banks of snow. No use to turn and run back—the ghost would chase him—and anyway he had to get to Dr. Geddes. Perhaps if he just trudged along quietly, he thought, without *seeming* afraid, he could just pass by this apparition and nothing would happen. So on he went.

In a minute he heard a voice say, "Is that Ben Doane?"

"Yes," said Ben.

"You're far from home this cold night!"

Then Ben saw that it was Bob Thurston, who lived on Brass's Hill. He had been to Barrington Head to buy a sack of flour and was carrying it home across his shoulders. Ben had not been able to see the man's head with the white sack of flour behind it against the banked white snow on the hill. Ben glanced at the man's feet. He was wearing heavy white wool spats, and the snow was up around his ankles.

It was not a headless and footless ghost! It was just good old Bob Thurston in his white spats, carrying home a sack of flour.

They chatted a moment or two. Then Ben said, "Mr. Thurston, did you ever see any ghosts around here? People say there's ghosts on Brass's Hill."

"No. Never saw anything worse than myself!"

SUNRISE

There is a nice old gentleman living in Halifax, Nova Scotia, who finds it hard to sleep all night. Sometimes, to ease his sleeplessness, he gets up and takes a little walk in the quiet streets.

One night he walked to a nearby cemetery and sat by his wife's grave for about an hour. Then, feeling drowsy, he got up to walk home and go to sleep in bed.

Just as he was coming out the cemetery gate, a young man turned the corner and came walking toward him. When he saw the old fellow bent over on his cane and stepping slowly out of the graveyard gate, he pointed his finger right at him.

"You go right back in there!" he said. "The sun is coming up in two minutes!"

A Scary Game

DEAD MAN

Dead Man is a game played by schoolchildren and college students just for the scary fun of it. Some of them know the game and have prepared the objects to be passed from hand to hand in the dark. The more there are who do *not* know the game, the more fun it is.

The players sit in a circle in the dark and speak in low, scary voices. No one can see. They can only hear and feel!

One says, "Here is the dead man's eye," and passes into the hand of the next player a peeled grape (or maybe a shelled clam).

After that has gone round the circle, someone else says, "Here is the dead man's hand," and passes into the hand of the next child an old cloth glove filled with wet sand or mud (or an ice-cold rubber glove filled with shaved ice).

"Here are the dead man's brains," says another player who passes on a soft squashy tomato.

Then (if the game lasts that long) another says, "These are the worms that crawled out of his skin," and passes on a handful of wet, slippery, cooked spaghetti.

As soon as someone screams the game is over. Lots of people scream.

This is a widespread and favorite game for Halloween parties and is used in school and college sorority and fraternity initiations to haze new members. Sometimes some luckless new boy or girl is made to eat the "worms" in the dark.

Somebody comes up with something new every time it is played. A dried chicken bone, for instance, can be produced as the old skeleton's finger; the bone called the pope's nose can be his nose bone. One player once remarked, as he handed it on, that it had fallen inside the corpse's skull and was hard to dig out! An old piece of wet or greasy fur can be presented as the dead man's hair, with an aside that he had a crew cut or wore it lanky—whichever is appropriate.

What else can you think up?

Notes and Bibliography

ABBREVIATIONS USED IN THE NOTES AND BIBLIOGRAPHY

BAEB	*Bureau of American Ethnology Bulletin*
DFML	*Dictionary of Folklore, Mythology, and Legend*
FCBCNCF	*Frank C. Brown Collection of North Carolina Folklore*
FFB	*French Folklore Bulletin*
JAF	*Journal of American Folklore*
MAFS	*Memoirs of American Folklore Society*
NCF	*North Carolina Folklore*
NMFR	*New Mexico Folklore Record*
ODNR	*Oxford Dictionary of Nursery Rhymes*
WF	*Western Folklore*

NOTES FOR TEACHERS AND PARENTS

The motif numbers are as given in Stith Thompson's *Motif Index of Folk Literature.*

Don't Worry. The motifs touched upon in this article are the ghostly vanishing hitchhiker (E332.3.3.1), ghost rides bus (E581.4) and disappears before it crosses bridge (E581.4.1). The ghostly hitchhiker at the bridge involves motif E332.1 and E332.33. The ghost ships are covered by motif E535.3.

Ghost guards treasure is motif E291; ghost prevents men from raising treasure is motif N576; not to speak while digging treasure is motif C401.3. Tom Surette's treasure-hunt tale is given here with his permission.

Ghost raised by whistling is motif E384.2. Ghost frightened by own reflection is motif K1715.1.2.

FAMOUS GHOSTS

White House Ghosts. This material is based on the facts as given in B. A. Botkin: *Sidewalks of America,* 183–187, citing Leslie Lieber: Legends of Ghosts in the White House, *This Week Magazine,* April 25, 1964, pp. 7, 31, 45, 50, United Newspaper Magazine Corporation, New York; also as given in Folklore in the News: Ghosts in the White House, *WF* 17:63–64.

Several traditional ghost-tale motifs apply to this material: ghost makes rapping noises (E402.1.5); ghost plays musical instrument (E554); ghost hunting something lost (E415.1); ghost of cat (E521.3); ghost identifying himself (E451.4.1).

Earl Gerald. This old legend of Earl Gerald and his return from the dead every seven years is told at length in Patrick Kennedy: *Legendary Fictions of the Irish Celts,* 153–155. Dead person visits earth every seven years is motif E585.1. The legend also belongs, of course, to the worldwide king asleep in the mountain tradition (motif D1960.2). There are countless legends of kings, chieftains, heroes, who sleep for centuries within a mountain or cave who are to arise and save their peoples at the moment of need.

Anne Boleyn. This story is based on the recorded histories and on Christina Hole: *Haunted England,* pp. 60, 61, 62. The motifs involved are: procession of the dead (E491), ghost carries head under arm (E422.1.1.4), ghost carries own head (E592.3). Phantom coach and horses is motif E535.1.

The music-hall song appeared in the 1930s on a 12-inch Riverside Record, #626, called *Ghost Ballads.* It was sung and made famous by Gracie Fields, Noel Coward, and Alec Templeton. The words can be found (but not the music), typed on a card, in the music division of the New York Public Library of the Museum of Performing Arts.

DON'T RUN

White Ghosts. This sharp bit of advice about what to do if you meet up with a white ghost was written by Anfey Goley, a little Aleut Eskimo girl, eleven years old. It was a school English-lesson exercise. *See* J. E. Ransom: Stories, Myths, and Superstitions of Fox Island Aleut Children, *JAF* 60:67.

Skull Race. This is a very old ghost-race story, reported by Zelia Nuttall: A Note on Ancient Mexican Folk-Lore, *JAF* 8:122. It is derived from the writings of Bernardino de Sahagún, Franciscan friar of Old Spain and famous missionary and historian in Mexico more than four hundred years ago.

Nobody Here But You and Me. This is one of the famous ghost-race tales. There are a hundred or more of them, told in Africa and the New World, wherever Negroes have settled. This one was told to Dr. Arthur H. Fauset in 1923, when he was collecting tales among Negroes in Philadelphia. The teller of this tale was a man from North Carolina. *See* Arthur H. Fauset: Tales and Riddles Collected in Philadelphia, *JAF* 41:542, #25.

Ghost converses with man running from him is motif J1495.1.

What's the Matter? This story, as given here, is expanded from a brief summary of it from New York State. *See* Louis C. Jones: New York Ghosts, *JAF* 57:240. It is still one more to be added to the hundreds of fear-test tales: staying in haunted house (motifs H1411 and H1411.1), known and told with innumerable variations in England, Scotland, Ireland, and the United States, especially in the southern United States among both blacks and whites. It is known also in India, Japan, the Cape Verde Islands, and among Greenland Eskimos. It also contains the famous ghost converses with man running from him motif (J1495.1).

THE KIND THAT WON'T STAY DEAD

Old Tom Comes Home. This is one of the twelve stories in the prize-winning entry entitled "Twelve Tall Tales from Wilkes County," published in *North Carolina Folklore* 10:3–10 (February 1972). The *North Carolina Folklore* journal (Raleigh, N. C.) announced, early in 1971, a prize contest for student-written folklore papers. Of the eight papers published, first prize went to Jerry D. Joines, a student at the University of North Carolina at Chapel Hill, for his "Twelve Tall Tales from Wilkes County," from which this one was published in *American Folklore Newsletter* 1:2 (1972). It is given here as written by Jerry D. Joines, who heard it from his father. It is reprinted with the kind permission of the author and *North Carolina Folklore.*

Ghost of cat is motif E521.3; ghost carries own head is E592.3.

'Tain't So. This story is condensed from the tale as told in Dr. John Bennet: *The Doctor to the Dead,* pp. 235–240. He cites Emmy Seabrook as informant. This is one from the famous collection of white and black tales collected by him over many years in the Charleston, South Carolina, and Sea Islands area.

TREASURE GHOSTS

One Handful. This story was told to me by Mr. Arthur Goodland of Georgetown, Guyana, in November 1972, as it was told to him by Mr. Ray Wilkins in 1966. Mr. Goodland saw the two stumps of wrists without hands.

The story has earmarks of true and widely diffused folk tradition. Ghost directs man to hidden treasure is motif E545.12, familiar in the ghost tales of England, the United States, Canada, and India. Treasure discovered through dream is motif N531, known throughout the British Isles and the United States, and occurring in FCBCNCF 1:693. It also occurs in the folktales of Iceland, Denmark, India, China, and there are Jewish and African Fjort variants. Hand(s) cut off for breaking tabu (motif C948.6) is cited in Dov Neuman's *Motif Index to Talmudic-Midrashic Literature.* Treasure chest breaks avaricious man's neck (motif Q272.2) is certainly analogous with this tale. It occurs in J. E. Keller's *Motif-Index of Mediaeval Spanish Exempla.* The more general avarice punished motif (Q272) turns up in Icelandic, Irish, Lithuanian, Spanish, Chinese, and Buddhist story, as well as in Maori, Tongan, and Tuamotu tales from the Pacific, and from Greenland Eskimo and African and West Indian black folktales.

The Supanaan River mentioned in the tale is a tributary of the Essequibo River, which runs through the center of Guyana 650 miles north from the Brazilian border into the Atlantic.

The silk-cotton tree is named for the silky floss that envelops its seeds. It is especially reverenced throughout the Guianas for various supernatural associations. (Among Surinam blacks, for instance, it is called the *god tree.*) In Guyana it sheds beneficence on all who reverence it. Treasure hidden in tree's roots is motif D2157.3.2.

Can't Rest. This story of the weary treasure-guarding ghost is reported from Wayne County, Missouri, by Vance Randolph: *Ozark Superstitions,* p. 220. Return from the dead to reveal hidden treasure is motif E371. Ghost laid when treasure is found is motif E451.5.

Blackbeard's Treasure. This story is based on two tales as reported in *FCBCNCF* 1:692–693. Such tales are still told with varying details by old people of that area.

Man killed and buried to guard treasure is motif N532; ghost prevents men from raising treasure is motif N576; ghost singing is motif E402.1.1.4. Treasure-finders always frightened away (motif N556) has analogs all over the United States and Canada, in Nova Scotia, Lithuania, and India.

The Tired Ghost. This story is reported by George Patterson: Notes on the Folk-Lore of Newfoundland, *JAF* 8:288.

Miss Olga Litowinsky of The Viking Press makes the amusing comment here that in these four treasure-ghost tales one man gets the treasure, one man almost gets some, one doesn't get any, and one old guardian ghost can't even give it away.

CAULD, CAULD

Cauld, Cauld, Forever Cauld. This pathetic little-boy ghost is still famous in Cumberland, but in general English legend he is often confused with the Cauld Lad of Hilton Hall (in Lancashire) who was a friendly but mischievous household spirit. Christina Hole differentiates between the two in her *Haunted England,* p. 7, as does also Henry Bett: *English Legends,* pp. 90–91. T. Keightley, *Fairy Mythology,* p. 296, tells the story of the Cauld Lad of Hilton. The revenant with ice-cold hands (motif E422.1.3) occurs in Danish, English, and United States ghost lore.

The Outside Man. These two stories about the Outside Man, written by Aleut Eskimo schoolchildren as an English-lesson exercise, are among those reported by J. Ellis Ransom: Stories, Myths, and Superstitions of Fox Island Aleut Children, *JAF* 60:63, 64.

I'm Coming up the Stairs. This is a widespread and common story that children love to tell each other in England, Canada, and the United States. As told here about Tilly, it is expanded from the very brief version reported to the Opies from a little girl twelve years old in Alton, England. *See* Iona and Peter Opie: *Lore and Language of Schoolchildren,* p. 36.

The Man on Morvan's Road. This story was given to me by Marion Robertson of Shelburne, Nova Scotia, to whom it was told by word of mouth by the Misses Allen of Shelburne. Dr. Helen Creighton mentions the ghost of Morvan's Hill in her *Bluenose Ghosts,* 171, and describes his appearing to a buckboard full of people in the road one night when they stopped to mend harness. The man leaned into the vehicle to peer into the faces of the people and then disappeared. The experience of the lone foot-traveler in Morvan's Road was told to me in the summer of 1972 by Mr. Ransom Wall of Shelburne.

A story almost identical with this is localized in Montgomery County, West Virginia. It is the story of a shadowy human figure that walks alongside night travelers in a certain lonely road, neither offering speech nor answering, and suddenly vanishing. It was reported by Dr. Samuel P. Bayard: Witchcraft, Magic, and Spirits on the Border of Pennsylvania and West Virginia, *JAF* 51:55.

Person meets ghost on road is motif E332.2, citing English, Canadian, and United States occurrences. Road ghosts; ghosts haunt roads is motif E272 and is known in Lapland, England, the United States (specifically New York, North Carolina, the Ozarks, and the Pennsylvania–West-Virginia border area), and also Canada, specifically Nova Scotia.

Staring at You. This story was told to me in April 1973 by Cecil Yarbrough of Burlington, North Carolina, who was one of the two little boys. The headless man by the creek or by the bridge (motif E422.1.1) turns up in the folk belief (black and white) of nearly every southern state. Compare *FCBCNCF* 1:683.

The Sea Captain at the Door. This story was first told to me by Marion Robertson, of Shelburne, Nova Scotia, in 1961, and again in the summer of 1972. It was a very vivid personal experience of her own. Ghost of drowned man leaves puddle of water where he stood is motif E544.1.3, citing only a United States reference, to which Nova Scotia can now be added. Ghosts of the drowned appear in wet or dripping clothes is motif E723.7.8. The drowned cannot rest is motif E414.

Grandpa Joe's Brother. This story was given to me in August, 1972 by Anne Wickens (Mrs. Arthur Wickens) of Bear Point, Nova Scotia. Her husband is Grandpa Joe's grandson. For explanation of the *wraith* or *forerunner,* see DON'T WORRY.

Bill Is with Me Now. This is a very old and very famous ghost story. As told here, it is condensed from the telling given by William Jones in *Credulities Past and Present,* pp. 87–89, citing Sir Walter Scott's *Letters on Demonology and Witchcraft,* London, 1884 (no page given).

The word *yard* as used in this story refers to a long cylindrical spar set crosswise of a ship's mast to support a square sail. A *yard-arm* is technically either end of a yard. The *slave-kettle* was a huge kettle formerly used on slave-trade ships for cooking food for the human beings being transported as slaves.

Tony and His Harp. This story was sent to me by Macdonald H. Leach from Raleigh, North Carolina. He has been to the house and heard the story, but he did not stay all night to hear the harp.

Ghost lore, no matter where it turns up, follows a pattern. Here again is the drowned man's ghost who leaves a small puddle of water on the floor (motif E544.3); ghost plays musical instrument is motif E554.

GHOSTLY THINGS

Crossing the Bridge. This small tale follows the story as told in "The Bridge That Wasn't There" in B. A. Botkin: *A Treasury of New England Folklore,* 345–346, reprinted from John Warner Barber: *Massachusetts Historical Collections . . . Relating to the History and Antiquities of Every Town in Massachusetts,* Dorr, Howland, and Company, Worcester, Mass., 1839, p. 73.

The story has become a strictly local legend in many widespread localities. It is found frequently, especially in New England, but Dr. Botkin reports a version from Indiana also in his *Treasury of American Anecdotes,* 224–225.

The tale takes two forms: (1) the traveler and his horse have just crossed a bridge which actually *was not there*—a ghost bridge which saved the lives of horse and rider; and (2) the impossible is seen to have been possible in the morning, for daylight reveals that the wise old sure-footed horse had crossed without fear on a remaining two-foot-wide stringer-beam. The two versions seem equally wonderful, but for this book we have chosen the ghost bridge. That horses can see ghosts and spirits is a well-known element of ghost lore and horse lore (motif E421.1.2).

The Ghostly Spools. This story is slightly expanded from the version told by Mrs. Charles Stone to Barbara Shuttleworth: Supernatural Folk Stories in the French-Canadian Tradition, *FFB* 7:3. Return from the dead to restore stolen goods is motif E352. Stories about ghosts returning from the dead to restore something stolen are known in England, Canada, the United States, Germany, the Scandinavian countries, and Persia.

Tick, Tick, Tick. This story is expanded from a brief report contributed by H. L. Taylor and edited by Rebecca Wolcott. *See* Items from New Castle, Delaware, *JAF* 51:92.

Pumpkin. This story is based on an old conjure tale from the black people of central Florida, collected by Zora Hurston. *See* Zora Hurston: Voodoo in America, *JAF* 44:403.

BOGEYS AND BUGABOOS

Jenny Green Teeth. Jenny Green Teeth is described in John Harland and T. T. Wilkinson: *Lancashire Folk-Lore,* p. 53, and in Thomas Keightley: *Fairy Mythology,* p. 296.

Baba Yaga. This famous Russian bogey is described in Y. M. Sokolov's *Russian Folklore,* 425, and in *DFML,* **100d.** See also the Baba Yaga tales in *Russian Fairy Tales,* pp. 76–78, 194–195, 363–365. Polish children have the same bogey, but her name is Jedza.

Nuinumma-Kwiten. This giant bogey and comfortless lullaby are reported by Theresa C. Brakeley in *DFML,* **804a.**

Pot-Tilter. Pot-Tilter is known to the Crow, Hidatsa, and Gros Ventre Indians of the North American Plains and is used especially as a child-frightener to keep children from wandering too far from home or leaving the villages without adult protection. Pot-Tilter is motif G331, citing Stith Thompson: *Tales of North American Indians,* 321, *n*157. See also *DFML,* 743a, 816c, **883a.**

Willie Winkie. Willie Winkie was originally a Scottish nursery character, taken over into English nursery lore. Later he migrated from the British Isles to the United States and Canada along with our Scottish and English ancestors.

The song was written by the Scottish poet, William Miller and was first published in the song collection entitled *Whistle-Binkie,* published by David Robertson, 1841. The song turns up in too many books to refer only to one. For brief comment, see *DFML,* 653d.

Raw Head and Bloody Bones. This horrifying bogey is mentioned in *Wyll the Deuyll,* about 1550 (perhaps by George Gascoigne). *See* Archer Taylor: Raw Head and Bloody Bones, *JAF* 69:114, continued on 175. This discussion also gives the source of the *old ouglie* (ugly) quotation as the play entitled *The Bugbears* (c. 1564 or 1565) citing B. J. Whiting: *Proverbs in the Earlier English Drama,* Cambridge, Mass., 1938. See also *FCBCNCF* 1:466; and *FCBCNCF* 7:155. Donald C. Simmons, in his Further Note on Raw Head and Bloody Bones, *JAF* 70:358, also mentions a quotation from *Wyll the Deuyll* and speculates on even more ancient sources, such as there having originally been two characters: Raw Head *and* Bloody Bones, who became merged into one, possibly in old pageants and morality plays.

WITCH LORE

The Black Cat's Eyes. This New Mexico story is one of a series of sixteen presented by Floy Padilla: Witch Stories from Tapia Azul and Tres Fulgores, *NMFR* 6:15. The author of this valuable article has written under a fictitious name, perhaps to avoid recognition by the witches she has exposed! Witches use eyes of animals to travel at night; leave own eyes at home is motif G249.10.1, citing only United States occurrence.

How to Become a Witch. This story is one of several local legends from Watauga County, North Carolina, based on the telling in *FCBCNCF* 1:648–649.

FAKES

Next Turn to the Right. This story is condensed from one of greater length about a stupid Hindu monk of Ceylon named Dandaka, in W. A. Clouston: *The Book of Noodles,* 158–160. Clouston bases his telling on the story from a Hindu text (title translated as *Thirty-Two Tales of Hindu Monks*), discussed in the journal *Orientaliste* (Kandy, Ceylon, 1884, p. 122). The tale was also told in Poggio Bracciolini's *Liber Facetiorum,* 1470, from which a number of other European jestbooks picked it up, among them the English *Tales and quicke answers* (1535) in P. M. Zall, ed.: *A Hundred Merry Tales and Other English Jestbooks of the Fifteenth and Sixteenth Centuries,* p. 287, #58. The tale contains two famous and widespread motifs: person made to believe that he is dead—J2311, and dead man speaks up—J2311.4. See also this motif in D. P. Rotunda: *Motif Index of the Italian Novella in Prose.*

Dr. Harold Courlander also reports a version of this tale, based on the same two motifs, from Eritrea, a province of Ethiopia: probably either of Indian or southern European provenience. This is a longer, locally elaborated story entitled "The Woodcutter of Gura," in Harold Courlander and Wolf Leslau: *Fire on the Mountain and Other Ethiopian Stories,"* Henry Holt and Company, New York, N.Y., 1950, pp. 19–23.

A Breath of Air. This brief anecdote comprises motif J2311.3—sham revenant comes up for air; it is one of the escapades of the fourteenth-century Turkish noodle, Hodscha Nasreddin. *See* A. Wesselski: *Hodscha Nasreddin* 1:206, #6, Weimar, 1911.

The Ghost on Brass's Hill. This is a family legend that I have heard told many times since I was a child. Young Ben Doane was my grandfather, who used to tell it about himself.

Sunrise. This story was told to me in the spring of 1972 by Donald M. Robertson of Shelburne, Nova Scotia. The aging gentleman who lives in Halifax is a long-time friend of his. He says the old man loves to tell this story on himself.

This book ends with a story called *Sunrise* because all ghosts are supposed to return to their graves at sunrise. Living man thought to be ghost is motif J1786; but of course we do not know whether it applies to this story or not. We do not know whether the young man really thought the old man was a ghost or whether he just thought it was a good joke.

A SCARY GAME

Dead Man. This game is too well known and widespread to cite any one reference.

BIBLIOGRAPHY

Samuel P. Bayard: Witchcraft, Magic, and Spirits on the Border of Pennsylvania and West Virginia, *JAF* 51: 47–59 (1938)

John Bennett: *Doctor to the Dead,* Rinehart and Company, New York, 1946

Henry Bett: *English Legends,* B. J. Batford, London and New York, 1952

B. A. Botkin: *Sidewalks of America,* Bobbs-Merrill Company, Indianapolis and New York, 1958

———: *A Treasury of New England Folklore,* Crown Publishers, New York, 1947

W. A. Clouston: *The Book of Noodles,* Elliott Stock, London, 1888

Ed Cray: Raw Head and Bloody Bones, *WF* 20:276 (1961)

Helen Creighton: *Bluenose Ghosts,* Ryerson Press, Toronto, 1957

Arthur H. Fauset: Tales and Riddles Collected in Philadelphia, *JAF* 41:529–557 (1928)

———: Folklore from Nova Scotia, *MAFS* 24 (1931)

Frank C. Brown Collection of North Carolina Folklore, vols. 1 and 7, Duke University Press, Durham, N.C., 1952 and 1964

Folklore in the News: Ghosts in the White House, *WF* 17:63–64 (1958)

John Harland and T. T. Wilkinson: *Lancashire Folk-Lore,* Frederick Warne and Company, London; Scribner and Company, New York, 1867

Christina Hole: *Haunted England,* B. T. Batsford, London and New York, 1951

Zora Hurston: Voodoo in America, *JAF* 44:317–417 (1931)

Louis C. Jones: Ghosts of New York, *JAF* 57:237–254 (1944)

William Jones: *Credulities Past and Present,* Chatto and Windus, London, 1898

Thomas Keightley: *Fairy Mythology* (rev. ed.), H. G. Bohn, London, 1850

Patrick Kennedy: *Legendary Fictions of the Irish Celts,* Macmillan and Company, London and New York, 1891

A. L. Kroeber: Handbook of the Indians of California, *BAEB* 78:207 (1925)

Maria Leach: Personal folklore files

———: Personal communications from: Mr. Arthur Goodland, Georgetown, Guyana; Macdonald H. Leach, Raleigh, N. C.; Marion Robertson and Donald M. Robertson, Shelburne, Nova Scotia; Mr. Thomas Surette, Yarmouth, N. S.; Mr. and Mrs. Ransom Wall, Shelburne, N.S.; Anne Wickens, Bear Point, N.S.; Cecil Yarbrough, New York.

———and Jerome Fried: *Dictionary of Folklore, Mythology, and Legend,* 2 vols., Funk and Wagnalls Company, New York, 1949–1950; 1-vol. ed., 1972

Zelia Nuttall: A Note on Ancient Mexican Folk-Lore, *JAF* 8:117–129 (1895)

Iona and Peter Opie: *Oxford Dictionary of Nursery Rhymes,* Clarendon Press, Oxford, 1951

———: *The Lore and Language of Schoolchildren,* Oxford University Press, London, 1960

Floy Padilla: Witch Stories from Tapia Azul and Tres Fulgores, *NMFR* 6:11–19 (1951–1952)

George Patterson: Notes on the Folk-Lore of Newfoundland, *JAF* 8:285–290 (1895)

Vance Randolph: *Ozark Superstitions,* Dover Publications, New York, 1964; 1st ed., Columbia University Press, New York, 1947

J. Ellis Ransom: Stories, Myths, and Superstitions of Fox Island Aleut Children, *JAF* 60:62–72 (1947)

D. P. Rotunda: *Motif Index of the Italian Novella in Prose,* Indiana Publications, Folklore Series, Indiana University Press, Bloomington, 1942

Russian Fairy Tales, trans. Norbert Guterman; Commentary by Roman Jakobson, Pantheon Books, New York, 1945

Barbara Shuttleworth: Supernatural Folk Stories in the French Canadian Tradition, *FFB 7,* #401:1–4 (1949)

Donald C. Simmons: A Further Note on Raw Head and Bloody Bones, *JAF* 70:358–359 (1957)

Y. M. Sokolov: *Russian Folklore,* Macmillan Company, New York, 1950

Tales and quicke answers, very merry and pleasant to rede, printed by Thomas Berthelet, London, 1535, in P. M. Zall, ed.: *A Hundred Merry Tales and Other English Jestbooks of the Fifteenth and Sixteenth Centuries,* University of Nebraska Press, Lincoln, 1963, pp. 239–322

Archer Taylor: Raw Head and Bloody Bones, *JAF* 69:114, cont. on 175 (1956)

H. L. Taylor and Rebecca Wolcott: Items from New Castle, Delaware, *JAF* 51:92 (1936)

Stith Thompson: *Motif Index of Folk Literature,* 6 vols., Indiana University Press, Bloomington, 1955–1958

———: *Tales of the North American Indians,* Harvard University Press, Cambridge, Mass., 1929

P. M. Zall. *See Tales and quicke answers . . .*